DOCTOR DAN
THE BANDAGE MAN

By HELEN GASPARD

Pictures by
CORINNE MALVERN

A GOLDEN BOOK • NEW YORK

This book is for Richard Peter

Dan is a busy fellow. He is always on the go.
But one day in a big back-yard cowboy fight he
fell and scratched his finger on his make-believe gun.

And what do you think the big cowboy did?
He cried.

"Boo hoo hoo," Dan cried. And he ran in the house to his mother.

    Now his mother was always glad to see Dan. But a
cowboy crying? How could that be?
    "Why, that's nothing to cry over," Mother said
when she saw the bright red spot.

"We'll wash it clean with soap and water and bandage it up, and it will be better than new."

And quick as a wink, it was!

Back went Dan to the cowboy fight. And all
the boys gathered around to see his new clean
bandage, too.

Next day Dan hitched up Spotty his pup to take
his sister Carly's doll for a ride.

But Spotty saw a cat he wanted to chase, and he forgot all about that doll.

Lickety split, Spotty started off!

The wagon tipped over. The doll tumbled out.
And Carly started to cry, "My baby hurt herself,"
because the doll had a bump on her head.

"This is nothing to cry over," said brother Dan. "I know just what to do."

So he led Spotty and Carly into the house. And he carried the hurt little doll himself, with a rather bad bump on her head.

"We'll wash it clean," said Dan.
And he did.
"We'll bandage it up." And he did that, too.

Dan opened the wrapper. He picked the bandage
out and held the two stiff pieces.

And zip! that bandage was on the doll's head.

"There!" smiled Dan. "She's better than new."
"Now," said Carly. "I want one, too."

"Are you hurt?" asked Dan.

"I don't know," Carly said, looking for a scratch.
And sure enough, she found one. It was a very tiny
scratch, and rather old, but it was a scratch just
the same.

Dan washed it clean and bandaged it up.
"Thank you," said Carly. "It's better than new."

"Woof!" said Spotty, and held up his paw.

Dan laughed. "I guess you must want a bandage, too."

So he put one on Spotty's paw.

Next day Daddy was home from work. He went out to mow the lawn. And what do you think? He cut his finger on a slippery-sharp lawn mower blade!

"Let me fix you up, Dad," said Dan. "I know what to do. We'll wash your finger clean and bandage it up, and it will be better than new."

Dad looked surprised, but he followed Dan. And
soon Dad wore a bandage, too.

"You're a handy fellow to have around," said Dad. And he shook Dan's hand. "I have a new name for you. We'll call you Doctor Dan, the Bandage Man." And they do to this day. So we will, too.